HIGHWAY OF HEROES

Kathy Stinson

With a foreword by the Chief of the Defence Staff,
General Walter Natynczyk, CMM, MSC, CD

Fitzhenry & Whiteside

Dedicated to Canada's soldiers and their families

"You have made unimaginable sacrifices in the name of justice and freedom.
Your families have done the same... Time eases the pain, but it never goes away...
You are not alone. We know the price you have paid... Know that Canadians share this
pain and pride with you."

—Her Excellency the Right Honourable Michaëlle Jean, CC, CMM, COM, CD Governor General and Commander-in-Chief of Canada (2005-2010).
From her speech at the first presentation of the Sacrifice Medal, November 12, 2008.

Foreword from the Chief of the Defence Staff, General Walter Natynczyk, CMM, MSC, CD.

On behalf of the men and women serving the Canadian Forces, it is an honour for me to lend my support to this meaningful tribute to the Highway of Heroes.

Our fallen comrades are proud soldiers, sailors, airmen, and airwomen who chose a life of service to Canada and of promoting peace and security. These men and women in uniform made the ultimate sacrifice in their desire to make a difference in the world on behalf of all Canadians.

The Highway of Heroes has become a symbol of Canadian patriotism and will be an everlasting demonstration of our nation's gratitude for the brave fallen men and women in uniform who made the solemn journey from Trenton to Toronto.

I wish to thank everyone who came out to pay their respects on the bridges and along the Highway of Heroes. Your presence has provided great comfort to the families of our fallen.

This book will serve as a reminder of the respect and dignity paid by everyday Canadians who lined the routes and bridges during the repatriation of our fallen comrades. Its powerful images will demonstrate how Canadians share the pain of grief with the families.

General W.J. Natynczyk, CMM, MSC, CD
Chief of the Defence Staff

One Family':

The plane has landed.

Huddled against the wind, a boy stands stiffly with his mother on the tarmac. He wants to stamp his cold feet, but he knows he has to stand still like the soldiers and other people who have gathered at the Canadian Forces Base in Trenton. Somewhere nearby a bagpiper begins a tune that sounds like crying.

The ceremony welcoming the boy's father back to Canada goes on for a long time. Someone is saying what a brave and caring soldier he was—how thoughtful, how generous, how kind. The boy would rather be hearing his dad saying, "Hey, bud! I'm home!"

Of course, if his dad had come home alive, the boy and his mom would be at an airport closer to home, far across the country. His dad might have had a medal pinned to his chest, like some of the soldiers here today. Instead, his coffin is draped with a flag of Canada.

The boy and his mom climb into a black car that will ride behind the hearse on its way to the coroner's office in Toronto. As the cars pass through the gates of CFB Trenton, the boy wishes he were back home playing ball hockey with his friends—and with his dad. He wishes his dad had thought less about the problems of people far away and more about what it would be like for his own kid if he went and got himself killed.

Along the sides of the road, groups of police officers, fire fighters, and paramedics stand at attention as if they're frozen there.

A group of people on a corner waves. The boy's mom waves back, but the boy clenches his hands tightly in his lap. He wishes the cars would drive faster. It's a long way to Toronto and they'll never get there at this speed.

The line of cars pulls onto the highway. The sky is heavy and grey. The fields beside the highway are brown and streaked with snow.

In the back seat of the car, the boy's mom offers him a candy. The boy unwraps it and pops it in his mouth. Sucking on it helps take away the sting in the back of his throat.

After a while, his mom pats his hand and points up ahead.

The bridge over the highway is crowded with people. The boy wonders where they are all going.

As the car is about to pass under the bridge, he realizes the people aren't going anywhere. They are standing still. Many are waving Canadian flags or holding them open over the railing.

Then there are empty fields, shivery trees,

and more empty fields.

A sign says "Winter Hazards."
It means to watch for icy patches
or blowing snow.

Not bombs.

At the next overpass, there are more people. Saluting. Waving flags. Fire trucks and school buses, cars and pickup trucks are parked on the bridge, too.

Leaning forward, the boy looks up. He thinks, *These people couldn't have all known my dad. Not this far from home.*

As the convoy continues along the highway, up and down hills and through woods, past a giant apple, barns, old shacks, and more boring fields, the boy begins watching for the next bridge…wondering…

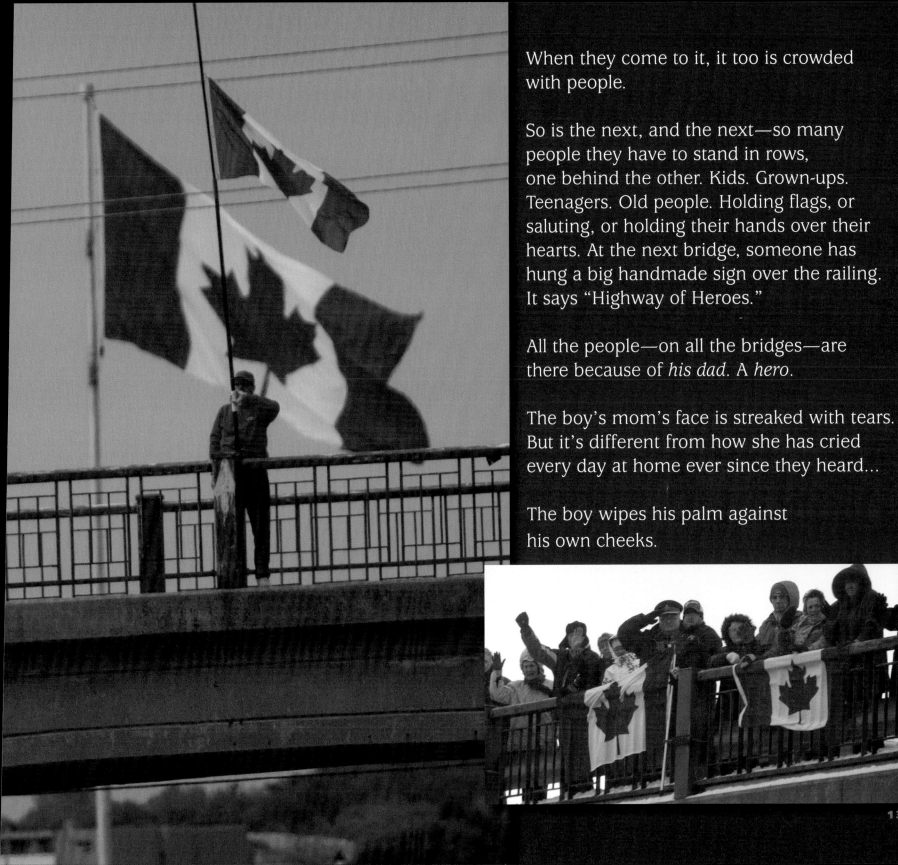

When they come to it, it too is crowded
with people.

So is the next, and the next—so many
people they have to stand in rows,
one behind the other. Kids. Grown-ups.
Teenagers. Old people. Holding flags, or
saluting, or holding their hands over their
hearts. At the next bridge, someone has
hung a big handmade sign over the railing.
It says "Highway of Heroes."

All the people—on all the bridges—are
there because of *his dad*. A *hero*.

The boy's mom's face is streaked with tears.
But it's different from how she has cried
every day at home ever since they heard...

The boy wipes his palm against
his own cheeks.

It's dusk when he sees an exit for Liberty Street. The people on that bridge are standing still and quiet. A large Canadian flag with a streetlight shining through it almost seems to glow.

"Liberty is like freedom, right?" the boy says.

"That's right," his mom answers.

*How many bridges have they passed? How many people have stood out there in the blowing cold,
even after snow began to fall? Since they left Trenton, not a single bridge has been empty.*

Is it like this whenever a dead soldier comes home? It must be.

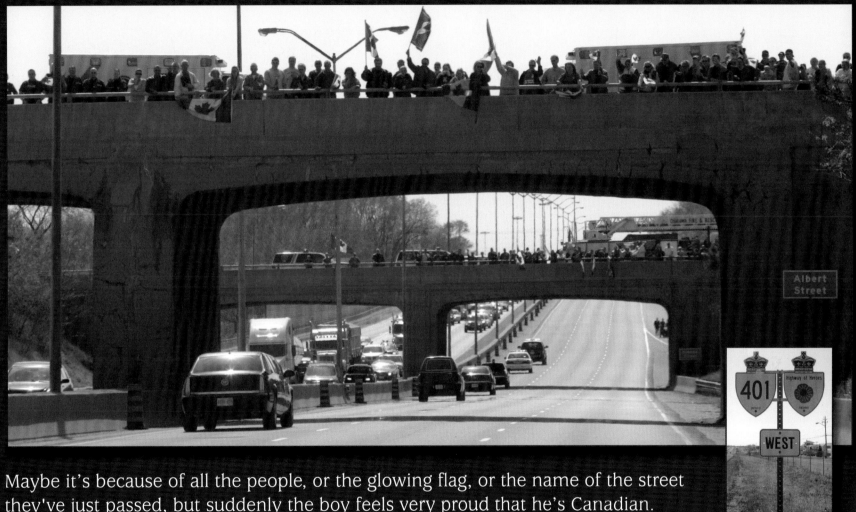

Maybe it's because of all the people, or the glowing flag, or the name of the street
they've just passed, but suddenly the boy feels very proud that he's Canadian.

The highway is quite wide now. High-rises and houses have begun to appear. As they
approach Toronto, the buildings in the distance begin to look bigger.

The trip has gone by faster than he thought it would. Or maybe it has just seemed faster.

Not long after the convoy leaves the highway, it heads along a downtown street. On sidewalks and street corners, more people are standing with flags or saluting as the cars pass.

The boy is feeling warmer now—warm enough to unzip his jacket.

As the hearse moves slowly between the tall buildings of downtown Toronto, some people walk along beside it. It's as if they are walking with his dad. *And with me*, the boy thinks.

A little girl holding her mom's hand, walking beside his car, waves to him and smiles.

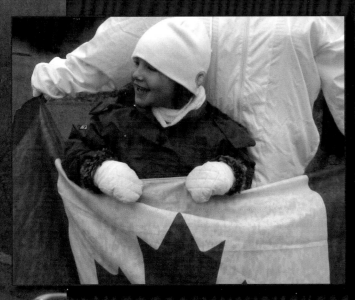

The boy waves back. His mom takes his other hand and squeezes it.

At the coroner's office, the boy gets out of the car. It feels good to stretch his legs. He feels lighter somehow than he did at the beginning of the ride down the highway. He feels less alone.

The boy will miss his dad forever. He knows that.
But he is proud to know that his dad was a hero.
He is proud that together they have traveled
Canada's Highway of Heroes.

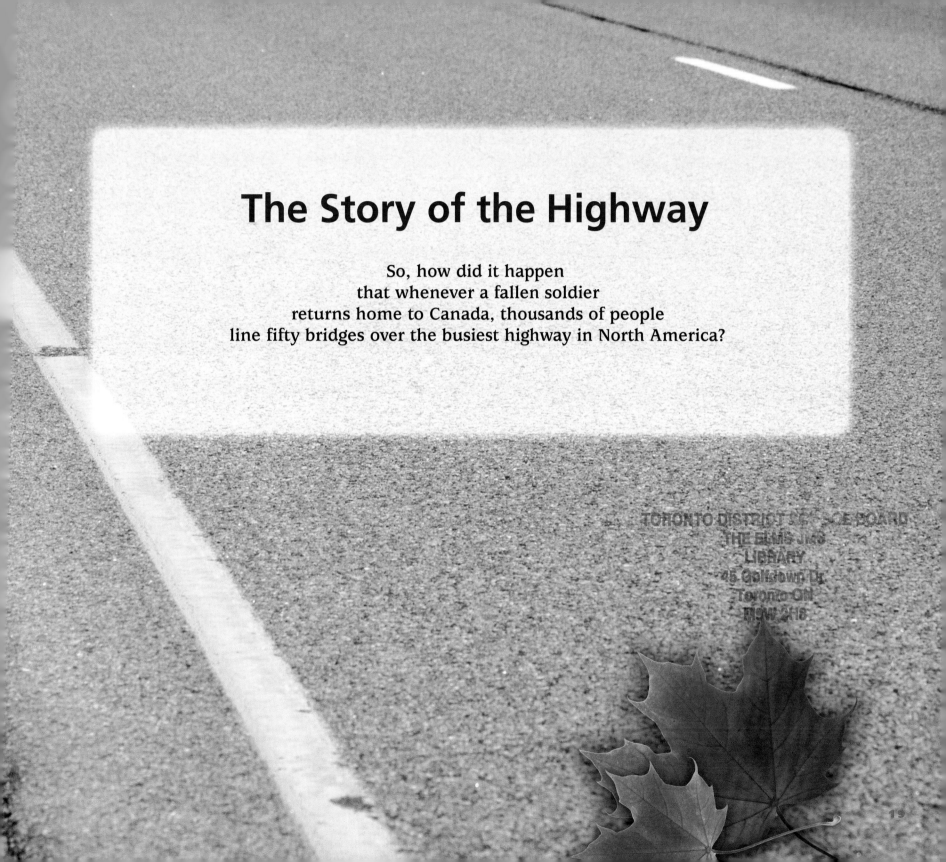

The Story of the Highway

So, how did it happen
that whenever a fallen soldier
returns home to Canada, thousands of people
line fifty bridges over the busiest highway in North America?

How indeed?

No one said anyone *had* to be there. No one organized people to gather. But one day in 2002, after hearing the news that fallen soldiers were returning home from Afghanistan, a number of people simply decided they should be present along the route the soldiers would be taken.

Each time another soldier was taken down the highway, more people showed up to pay their respects—young and old and from all walks of life. Newspapers reported what was happening. In the midst of sadness was an opportunity to tell a feel-good story. Then more people came. And more.

Why did people gather on the bridges over the highway?

They wanted to say "Thank you," to those who had sacrificed their lives. They wanted to say to grieving families, "We're sorry for your loss. We appreciate what your loved ones did."

"We come every time. You have to, really."*

"Our son is in Afghanistan right now, in the same exact unit. It really hits close to home—that could be us down there (in the procession). I read about (the deaths) in the news, and the bottom just sort of sinks out of your stomach."*

Repatriation simply means "returning to your home country."

Three RCMP officers who were killed in 2010 while serving in Haiti during the earthquake were honoured along the Highway of Heroes.

An **autopsy** is an operation that helps to determine officially how a person has died.

Route of Heroes
Bloor St E

Highway of Heroes

SUPPORT OUR TROOPS

How did that stretch of road come to be named "Highway of Heroes"?

In 2007 Joe Warmington, a writer for the Toronto Sun, started calling the section of the 401 that the military convoys traveled "the Highway of Heroes." That gave Pete Fisher, a writer and photographer for SunMedia out of Cobourg, the idea for an article which said, more or less, "Hey, we should make that name official."

Pete Fisher's article was picked up by national newspapers. Soon Jay Forbes of London, ON, started an online petition. Over 60,000 people signed it.

The 172 km stretch of Highway 401 from Glen Miller Rd. in Trenton to the 404/Don Valley Parkway in Toronto was officially renamed Highway of Heroes in September 2007. The route along the Don Valley Parkway through the city to the Coroner's Office on Grenville St. was named the Route of Heroes in June 2010.

Why are the heroes brought to CFB Trenton and then to the Chief Coroner's Office in Toronto, even if they are from other cities and provinces across Canada?

A repatriation ceremony is held for the heroes and their families at the Canadian Forces Base in Trenton. They are then taken by military escort to Toronto, where the chief coroner will perform an autopsy.

Who are the heroes who travel the Highway?

- Canadian soldiers who die overseas
- Canadian journalists who die while working to tell their stories
- and other Canadians who die while serving on missions overseas

CANADIAN SOLDIERS IN AFGHANISTAN

The heroes who inspired the first Highway tributes were coming home from Afghanistan.

Why were Canadians sent to fight in Afghanistan?

On September 11, 2001, al-Qaeda terrorists attacked the World Trade Center in New York and the Pentagon in Washington, D.C. Thousands of people were killed. The Afghan government at the time, the Taliban, had been allowing al-Qaeda leader Osama Bin Laden and his followers to live in Afghanistan as "guests." When the international community asked the Taliban government to give up Bin Laden and stop harbouring his terrorist group, the government refused.

In an effort to combat terrorism, many countries from around the world sent troops to remove the Taliban government from power. This was the beginning of the current war in Afghanistan.

Even though the Taliban was defeated and a new government was elected, there was still lots for Canadian soldiers and other aid workers to do. After years of war that pre-dated 9/11, the country needed rebuilding. After years of drought, its people needed help. And the Taliban and its supporters—considered to be a threat to the safety of ordinary Afghan citizens as well as other countries—did not go away quietly for long.

What have Canadian soldiers done in Afghanistan?

The new Afghan government has needed help from Canada and many other countries in order to establish peace and provide its citizens with everything that they need. Canada's military has helped the new government by:

- defending the Afghan government by fighting anti-government forces, including insurgent groups who support the Taliban;
- seizing weapons and removing land mines and bombs from places where they could blow up and hurt innocent people;
- delivering humanitarian aid, including medical supplies and other basic necessities, into dangerous areas;
- helping train the Afghan army, police force, and border officials so they can better keep Afghan citizens safe.

Canadian soldiers have also helped to protect non-military organizations so that they can accomplish important tasks including:

- repairing an important water system to help provide people with safe drinking water;
- building roads to give ordinary people safer routes to places they need to go;
- setting up health care programs;
- establishing a justice and court system to uphold law and order;
- creating jobs for Afghan citizens so that they can look after their families and improve their country's economy;
- building and repairing schools so more Afghan children can learn to read, write, and become responsible citizens when they grow up.

Andrew Eykelenboom was a 23-year-old who liked camping, fishing, snowboarding, and surfing. When he was serving as an army medic in Afghanistan, his mother asked what she could send him. He said, "I don't need anything. The people here do. Send me things for the kids. They don't have anything... Street people in Canada have more than anybody in the villages I've been in." Andrew was killed by a suicide bomber in 2006. After his death, his family set up a fund to benefit the children of Afghanistan.

An **insurgent** is a rebel who revolts against an established form of government or civil authority.

> *"It's hard to describe what it meant to me, to have so many people—complete strangers—standing tall and saluting my son. There are no words, but I want to thank them from the bottom of my heart for respecting my son."* *

Darlene Cushman, mother of Darryl Caswell who was killed by a roadside bomb in 2007

ON THE HIGHWAY AGAIN

Most people—inside and outside of Canada—think of Canadians as somewhat reserved and only quietly patriotic. So the open, heartfelt and spontaneous expression of support that takes place along the Highway of Heroes has taken many by surprise.

Are there other ways Canadians honour those who are killed or wounded in service to their country?

- Some hang yellow ribbons on trees, a tradition that has long welcomed loved ones home. Yellow ribbons are also displayed on bumper stickers and fridge magnets as a show of troop support.
- Starting in 2009, Canadian soldiers killed or wounded in Afghanistan have been awarded the Sacrifice Medal. The soldier's name and rank is engraved along the bottom.

Pete Fisher, the journalist who helped to name the Highway of Heroes, created a slideshow tribute.

Musician Bob Reid wrote a song in the basement of his Toronto bungalow.

To see the slideshow and hear the song, visit this book's website at
www.fitzhenry.ca/highwayofheroes

HAM radio operators William Skuta, Doug Eddy, and Joe Stratton have attended over 100 bridge gatherings.

> *"Thank you for bringing light and hope to people who have long known only darkness and despair."*
> —Right Honourable **Stephen Harper**, Prime Minister of Canada at the first Sacrifice Medal presentation

A NOTE FROM THE AUTHOR

In an ideal world, no more fallen soldiers would travel the Highway of Heroes with their grieving families. Sadly, it is not a perfect world. At least we can be sure that whenever another soldier and his or her family make that trip, Canadians will again line up along the route to share their grief and their pride.

This book is my way of standing alongside those on the bridges over the Highway. It's my way of saying thank you to soldiers, journalists, and others for doing what they can to make a positive difference in the world. It's my way of paying my respects to families who have lost and will lose loved ones—wherever and whenever they may serve. I thank Cathy Sandusky for giving me the idea to write it and those who gave us permission to include photos from personal collections.

Not all Canadians returning home from war zones travel the Highway of Heroes. Many come home alive, but they have experienced horrors most people in Canada—the lucky ones anyway—cannot even imagine. The returning soldiers may be injured physically. They may be deeply troubled by what they have seen and heard for a long time after their return to the relative calm and safety of Canada. Those soldiers are no less heroic than the ones who travel the Highway of Heroes. They need support too, and so do their families. That's why army captain Wayne Johnston set up woundedwarriors.ca, a charity that offers that support.

The world is full of heroes, people doing what they can to help make life better for others—often so quietly that not many people even know what they're up to. If you know someone like that, I hope you'll tell others about them—by making a photo album or slideshow, or by writing a song, a book, a story for a newspaper or magazine, or a blog post. If you don't have your own blog, you can send your story to me and I'll be happy to post it on mine.

Kathy Stinson

Out of respect for those whose lives will be sacrificed after publication of this book, a list of heroes who have traveled the Highway has not been included. For an up-to-date list and information about each hero, please visit www.fitzhenry.ca/highwayofheroes or the Canadian Forces website.

Published in Canada by Fitzhenry & Whiteside, 195 Allstate Parkway, Markham, Ontario L3R 4T8
Published in the United States by Fitzhenry & Whiteside, 311 Washington Street, Brighton, Massachusetts 02135

www.fitzhenry.ca   godwit@fitzhenry.ca

10 9 8 7 6 5 4 3 2

National Library of Canada Cataloguing in Publication Data, and U.S. Publisher Cataloging-in-Publication Data
(Library of Congress Standards) is on file ISBN 978-1-55455-182-8.

Fitzhenry & Whiteside acknowledges with thanks the Canada Council for the Arts, and the Ontario Arts Council for their support
of our publishing program. We acknowledge the financial support of the Government of Canada through the
Book Publishing Industry Development Program (BPIDP) for our publishing activities.

Canada Council   Conseil des Arts
for the Arts   du Canada

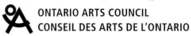

ONTARIO ARTS COUNCIL
CONSEIL DES ARTS DE L'ONTARIO

Cover and interior design by Kerry Plumley
Cover concept by Cheryl Chen
Printed in Canada

Photo Credits
All photos courtesy of Peter Fisher, QMI Agency with the following exceptions:
Frontpaper photo courtesy of The Canadian Press/Fred Chartrand
Photo of Canadian Sacrifice Medal courtesy of the Department of National Defence, Directorate of Honours & Recognition
p. 7   *Highway of Heroes sign* courtesy of Cathy Sandusky
p. 14   *Bridge supporters with fire truck* courtesy of Christie Harkin
           Liberty St. sign courtesy of Cathy Sandusky
p. 15   *401/Highway of Heroes sign* courtesy of Cathy Sandusky
p. 17   *Girl with flag* courtesy of Christie Harkin
p. 20   *Supporters with flags on street* courtesy of William Yum
p. 22   *Highway of Heroes decal* courtesy of Francesco Paonessa
           Supporters on bridge courtesy of Jennifer Murphy
p. 24   *Soldiers with flag of Quebec* courtesy of William Yum
p. 25   *Aircraft gunner* courtesy of The Canadian Press/Louie Palu
           Military camp courtesy of The Canadian Press/AP/David Guttenfelder
           Maps of world and Afghanistan courtesy of the University of Texas Libraries, The University of Texas at Austin
p. 26   *Dentists with Afghan man* courtesy of Sgt. Alain Belhumeur
           Soldier with children in Kandahar courtesy of Cpl. Simon Duchesne (Photo AR2008-Z136-07, Combat Camera/National
           Defense, reproduced with the permission of the Minister of Public Works and Government Services, 2010)
p. 27   *Soldier with children* courtesy of The Canadian Press/Bill Graveland
p. 28   *Girl with bear* courtesy of Tom Rutledge
           Family on bridge and *Three longtime supporters* courtesy of Francesco Paonessa
Endpaper photo courtesy of The Canadian Press/Louie Palu

Sources
*Quotes from pages 20, 21, and 28 can be found at http://www.thestar.com/news/ontario/article/550585
Stein, Janice Gross, and Eugene Lang. *The Unexpected War: Canada in Kandahar.* Toronto: Penguin Canada, 2008.
http://www.mapleleafweb.com/features/canada-afghanistan-military-and-development-activities#military
http://www.gg.ca/document.aspx?id = 13368